CLICK, CLACK, Quackity-Quack

An Alphabetical Adventure

by doreen cronin
and
betsy lewin

atheneum books for young readers

For my bunnies
—D. C.

To Julia. Welcome to the world.
—B. L.

Visit us at www.abdopub.com

Spotlight, a division of ABDO Publishing Company, is a school and
library distributor of high quality reinforced library bound editions.

Library bound edition © 2006

Atheneum Books for Young Readers
An imprint of Simon & Schuster Children's Publishing Division
1230 Avenue of the Americas, New York, New York 10020
Text copyright © 2005 by Doreen Cronin
Illustrations copyright © 2005 by Betsy Lewin
Book design by Ann Bobco
The text for this book is set in Filosofia.
The illustrations for this book are rendered in brush and watercolor.
Manufactured in the United States of America
First Edition
10 9 8 7 6 5 4 3 2
Library of Congress Cataloging-in-Publication Data
Cronin, Doreen.
Click, clack, quackity-quack: an alphabetical adventure / Doreen Cronin ;
illustrated by Betsy Lewin. —1st ed.
p. cm.
Summary: An assortment of animals gathers for a picnic.
ISBN-13: 978-0-689-87715-5
ISBN-10: 0-689-87715-3 (hc) 1-59961-089-2 (reinforced library bound edition)
[1. Picnicking—Fiction. 2. Animals—Fiction. 3. Alphabet.] I. Lewin, Betsy, ill.
II. Title.
PZ7.C88135Ck 2005
[E]—dc22 2004020212

a Animals awake

b beneath blue blankets.

Clickety-clack!

Duck dashing,

eggs emptying.

f Flippity-flip!

Goats
grooming,

g

h

hens
helping,

i inchworms inching.

j Jumpity-jump!

Kittens kicking,

leaping,

licking.

m Mice munching,

n nibbling nibbles.

Only one pig peeking.

r

Rain raining,

s

sheep sleeping.

t Tippity-toe

u under umbrellas.

V Vroom!

W

Watermelons
waiting.

marks the picnic spot.

Yawns yawning!

Z z z z z

ZZZZZZZZZZ.

doreen cronin is the author of the *New York Times* bestsellers *Duck for President*; *Giggle, Giggle, Quack*; and *Diary of a Worm*. Her first book, *Click, Clack, Moo: Cows That Type*, was named a Caldecott Honor Book. She lives in New York City with her husband, Andrew, and daughter, Julia, who loves to hear the ABCs read out loud.

betsy lewin is the Caldecott Honor–winning illustrator of *Click, Clack, Moo: Cows That Type* and its sequels, *Giggle, Giggle, Quack* and *Duck for President*, in addition to a number of other picture books, including *So, What's It Like to Be a Cat?* and *Two eggs, please*. She lives in Brooklyn, New York.